W9-BLN-118

Felicia Bond

Wake Up, Vladimir

Thomas Y. Crowell   New York

E
B

5179

For Ellen

Wake Up, Vladimir
Copyright © 1987 by Felicia Bond
Printed in the U.S.A. All rights reserved.
1 2 3 4 5 6 7 8 9 10
First Edition

Library of Congress Cataloging-in-Publication Data
Bond, Felicia.
   Wake up, Vladimir

   Summary: Vladimir Groundhog runs away from home in
late autumn and, after a long winter's sleep, wakes up,
scares away a monster and runs home never to leave again.
   [1. Woodchuck—Fiction] I. Title.
PZ7.B63666Wak 1987   [E]   84-45342
ISBN 0-690-04452-6
ISBN 0-690-04453-4 (lib. bdg.)

Late in autumn, when no one was looking,
Vladimir Groundhog stole away from his mother
and father and their home in the hills.

For many days they had been eating, and eating, and eating.

Then it was time for their long winter's sleep.
Vladimir did not want to sleep.

Run away, Vladimir, said a voice in his head.

Run away, Vladimir. Run away, run away.

The day passed, and it grew colder.

Vladimir burrowed a hole much like the one he had lived in.

Pebbles and dirt and scrambled-up twigs soon covered the door to Vladimir's house.

Winter came.

Inside the earth, Vladimir fell deeply asleep.
Sleep, Vladimir. Sleep, sleep.

Day and night

Vladimir dreamed…

WILLIAMSBURG METHODIST CHURCH
LIBRARY

through snow...

and wind...

until at last

the air grew warm

and winter had passed.

Wake up, Vladimir. Wake up, wake up.

Vladimir climbed out of his burrow.

A monster loomed before him.

Vladimir jumped, and shouted as loud as he could,

and the monster went away.

Go home, Vladimir. Go home, go home.

Vladimir ran to his home in the hills.

"Time to get up!" he said.

He told his mother and father of his dream
and the monster he had seen.

And he never ran away again.